WAIT FOR ME

Molly did not know what she planned to do exactly. She didn't want to go to school to Mrs. P. Lear's class. That was certain. She didn't want to see Amy and Lisa and their new best friend, Priscilla. She didn't want to stay at home all day with no one to speak to but Flips and Morgan, who at that moment lay curled and purring on her stomach.

She could hear her mother on the telephone and then she heard the sharp click of her high heels.

"Mary Christine," she said in quite a cross voice. "I know you're here." She opened the closet door. "Molly?" She was walking around the bedroom. "Please, Molly," she said. And suddenly the rose flounce of the bedspread lifted, and there was her mother, peering under the bed at Molly and Morgan.

"How did you know where to find me?" Molly asked.

"You are my daughter," her mother said. "I just knew."

Susan Shreve

WAIT FOR ME

Illustrated by Diane de Groat

A BEECH TREE PAPERBACK BOOK • NEW YORK

The Library of Congress has cataloged the Tambourine Books edition of
Wait for Me as follows:

Shreve, Susan Richards. Wait for me / by Susan Shreve;
illustrated by Diane de Groat—1st ed. p. cm.
Summary: As she begins fifth grade, Molly feels left behind by her older
sisters and brother and neglected by her former best friends.
ISBN 0-688-11120-3 (trade)
[1. Self-reliance—Fiction. 2. Brothers and sisters—Fiction.
3. Family life—Fiction. 4. Schools—Fiction.]
I. De Groat, Diane, ill. II. Title
PZ7.S55915Wai 1992 [Fic]—dc20 91-30233 CIT AC

First Beech Tree Edition, 1994.
ISBN 0-688-13622-2

To Katie, of course

WAIT FOR ME

Chapter One

Molly Lottmann was born too late.

She was born in May—May 7, 1979, to be exact—six years and four days after Sarah, who was in high school and lately spoke only in French.

"Bonjour, mes chéris," Sarah would call from the downstairs hall when she came home from school. *"Ça va?"*

"Please," Molly would beg her sister, "talk to me the right way."

But Sarah would simply throw her slender arms in the air and flounce into the kitchen.

"Je ne comprends pas, ma chérie," she'd say. And she would sit down at the kitchen table for her usual snack of raw carrots and cauliflower and broccoli, which was all she ate in order to re-

main thin as a piece of paper in her new short, short black knit skirt.

Molly had been born in the afternoon at Hollybridge Hospital in Medford, Massachusetts, four years, three months, and eleven days after Benjamin, who was captain of the baseball team at Lake Shore Junior High. Since the first day of junior high, when he pulled his baseball cap down over his eyes and took the L4 bus to Lake Shore, he had stopped speaking English.

"Uh uh rum rum, *yeah*," Benjamin would say from underneath his baseball cap.

"Benjamin isn't normal any longer," Molly told her father sadly.

"Speak English, Benjamin, if you remember the language," Mr. Lottmann would say crossly to Benjamin. "You sound like a gorilla."

"All boys Benjamin's age sound like gorillas, darling," Mrs. Lottmann said to Mr. Lottmann. "Pay no attention."

"You used to tell me your secrets about girls, do you remember?" Molly said one day, following Benjamin to the L4 bus stop.

"Yeah. Well, maybe, but now I'm too old for secrets and I don't like girls." On Clivedon

Avenue he met up with his friend Petie, and they took giant steps to the bus stop, leaving Molly panting far behind.

According to her babybook, Molly had been born on a Thursday, exactly two years to the hour after Ellie, with whom Molly had been the best of friends until Ellie started seventh grade. Then she began to wear bright plum lipstick and turquoise eye shadow and stopped speaking to anyone at all.

"Please," Molly would say to Ellie from the door to her bedroom, which was as far as she was allowed to go in Ellie's room, "can I borrow your red sweater for Sally's birthday?"

Ellie was looking at her eyelashes in the full-length mirror on her closet door, but Molly could see perfectly well the black expression on her once beloved sister's face.

"No," Ellie said. "You can't."

Molly's eyes filled with tears.

"You used to let me borrow your red sweater."

"Well, I don't anymore."

Everything used to be different for Molly in the Lottmann family. As far back as she could

11

remember, she had been happy as kittens to be last in line, the adorable baby of the Lottmann clan, prized and cherished and adored above all.

She was small for her age—ten years and four months on September 7, the first day of fifth grade—with a ring of black curls around her face.

"French poodle fur," Benjamin had said to her.

She had tiny dark dots for eyes and until recently a round face, a round belly, and round short legs.

"Baby fat," Sarah had said sweetly when she used to speak English. "You will lose it soon."

"And then she won't be an adorable baby any longer," Ellie had said. "Just ordinary Molly."

Ellie had been right. Now the baby fat was melting off like butter, her legs were thinner and longer, the bones in her cheeks showed through the flesh, and her sisters and brother had abandoned her like an old doll no longer loved.

"Nobody plays with me any longer. Have

you noticed?" Molly said to her mother one afternoon just before fifth grade started in September. "Sarah's always out and Benj's at sports and Ellie only speaks when Daddy makes her."

"You'll have to begin to make your very own life, Molly," Mrs. Lottmann said.

"I used to have my own life and it was right here with Sarah and Benjamin and Ellie," Molly said sadly. "Now they won't even wait for me."

"Wait for me," Molly would call in the morning from her bedroom, lying on her belly looking under the bed for her lost tennis shoe.

"Hurry up," Benj would call back, but by the time she got downstairs with one tennis shoe on and the other under her arm, Benj had already left for school and Ellie, sour as pickles, was just on her way.

"Wait for me, please, Ellie," Molly said, putting on her other tennis shoe.

"Can't," Ellie said, leaving by the back door. "You haven't even had breakfast yet."

"Will you wait for me to walk to school?"

Molly asked Sarah when she came downstairs in her skinny black skirt.

"My ride's here, Molly," Sarah said, grabbing a banana and flying out the back door for her ride with Josh Truitt in his tiny red car.

"*Au revoir, ma famille*," she called. "*Je vous adore.*"

"I hate Sarah," Molly said glumly to her mother, who was clearing up the breakfast dishes, half-dressed for work at Bronson and Bronson where she was a divorce lawyer.

"We don't hate," Mrs. Lottmann said.

"I do," Molly replied, and left for her first day of school at Lake Shore Elementary, walking the whole seven and a half blocks alone, which she had never in all her five years at elementary school had to do before. Either Benjamin or Sarah or Ellie or all of them had always walked Molly straight to the red front door.

Life at the Lottmann home had changed for Molly the summer before fifth grade. It had changed in fact on one beautiful Sunday in late June when Mr. Lottmann decided, at the last moment, to take the family on an all-day canoe trip down Barton Creek. Sarah had said she absolutely wouldn't go unless Josh Truitt, her new boyfriend, was invited. Ellie said she wouldn't be in a canoe with Josh Truitt because he was a creep and certainly she wouldn't go at all unless she got to canoe with Benjamin and without Molly. She said it right there in front of Molly so harshly, Mrs. Lottmann took Molly on her lap and kissed her hair.

"That was unkind," she said to Ellie.

But the damage was done. Molly leapt up from her mother's lap, put her cereal dish in the sink, ran upstairs, and cried into the long fluffy fur of Morgan, the old tabby cat.

She waited.

No one came after her. Nobody called upstairs to see if she were all right. No one even cared.

She heard them rustling in the kitchen, chattering back and forth, happy as clams in her absence. So she washed her face, blew her nose, and went back downstairs just as Sarah was suggesting that Molly go for the day to Aunt Martha's and play with her cousins.

"I will not," Molly said. "I am going canoeing with everybody else." She sat down at the table. "In the same canoe as Ellie."

Ellie gave Benjamin her "Oh, no" look but Benjamin was, as usual, underneath his baseball cap and didn't respond.

"Then, darling," Mrs. Lottmann said, running her hands through Molly's hair, "once we're on the trip, you must promise not to hold us up as you sometimes do."

"I won't," Molly said. "I don't. Ellie holds us up with her lipstick."

But upstairs she couldn't find her sneakers and then the laces broke and her blue shorts, the only ones she did not feel self-conscious wearing, had a rip in the seat. All of the Lottmanns were already in the car and bad tempered when Molly finally dashed out of the house. And that's the way things went all summer.

"Wait for me," Molly would call when Benj and Ellie went swimming at the community pool, but she couldn't find her bathing suit so they left without her, and she was afraid to walk alone because she had to pass the house (on Fessenden Street) of Bean Barrows, who was mean to girls.

"Wait for me," Molly would call when Sarah said, "Anyone want to go to the movies with Josh and me?" But by the time she found her allowance and her favorite yellow skirt, Sarah and Benj and Ellie were already on their way down Clivedon Avenue in Josh's red car, so Molly was left at home to watch television in the den with Morgan and Flips, the basset hound.

And so it went for Mary Christine Lottmann, called Molly, all summer long until the beginning of fifth grade when things simply got worse.

Chapter Two

The first day of fifth grade in Mrs. P. Lear's class was the most terrible day in Molly's life.

"The worst you can remember?" her mother asked that night at dinner.

"I can remember all of the bad days of my life and this one was the worst," Molly said.

"Not as bad as the day I ran into a tree with my bicycle and got a concussion," Benj said.

"Or when I had pneumonia and almost died," Ellie said with a satisfied smile. "Do you remember that Mommy?"

"Of course I remember that," Mrs. Lottmann said.

"Well, today didn't happen to you," Molly said to Ellie. "And today was terrible."

"*Très terrible*," Sarah shook her head. "*Pauvre petite* Molly."

"Even you said Mrs. P. Lear was the worst teacher in the world," Molly said.

"That is true," Sarah agreed. "Mrs. P. Lear is the rock bottom when it comes to teachers."

"But she's the teacher you have, Molly, so you'll have to make the best of it," Mr. Lottmann said.

Mr. Lottmann was always talking about making the best of bad situations. It drove everybody crazy, even reasonable Sarah.

"Now," Mrs. Lottmann said, brushing the hair off Molly's forehead, "tell me everything that happened to you today, Moll, step by step." And Molly did.

The first news Molly had early on the morning of September 7 was that Mrs. P. Lear, the witch, instead of Mr. Williams, the great, was going to be her fifth-grade teacher every single day for nine months until after she was eleven years old. Then she walked into the dreaded classroom, took her seat next to Billy Eaton, who was the fastest runner in fifth grade, and discovered with an awful sinking feeling in her stomach that not only did she have Mrs. P. Lear, but neither one of her best friends in the world would be in her fifth grade. She was going to be absolutely and completely alone.

Since the first day of kindergarten, Molly had had two best friends. They were a team. The Three Bears, they called themselves. First there was Amy Brooks, a round sugar cookie of a girl with rose-red hair and pink cheeks— then Lisa van der Mer, pole thin with slender yellow pigtails down her back, the best girl athlete in the whole grade, faster at running even than the boys—and Molly, the youngest of the three by six months and the smallest. Amy was the mother bear, fussing over Molly and Lisa like a plump hen. Serious competitive Lisa was the Daddy bear. And Molly was the adorable baby.

"Always the baby in the family," Mrs. Lott-mann said to Molly one morning after Lisa and Amy had slept over.

"I hate being the baby," Molly said, but the fact was she loved the warm and cozy safety of her life as the smallest and the youngest and the most loved.

*   *   *

At recess on the first day of fifth grade, after the bad news of Mrs. P. Lear, and language arts, and social studies, and music, Molly rushed outside as soon as the bell rang to look for Lisa and Amy in the place where they always met to tell secrets—under the weeping willow tree. She ran down the back steps of Lake Shore Elementary. There they were, sitting exactly where they always sat under the willow, barely visible through the leaves. But they were not alone. Seated between them was a girl Molly had never seen before, a very small girl with short brown hair done in ribbons, certainly too young to be in the fifth grade.

Molly felt suddenly strange. She walked over and slid down next to Amy.

"Hello," she said softly.

"Oh, hi, Moll," Amy said. "This is Priscilla. What is your last name?" she asked the brown-haired doll.

"James," the little girl said.

"She's new this year," Amy said.

"In what grade?" Molly asked, hoping she would say first or second.

"In our class," Lisa said.

23

"Then you must have Mr. Williams," Molly said, although of course she already knew.

"We all have him," Lisa said.

"He's really wonderful," Amy said.

"I know. That's what everybody says," Molly said. "Well, I don't have him."

"I'm really sorry you have Mrs. P. Lear," Amy said.

"Poor Molly," Amy said to Priscilla James. "She has the worst teacher in the whole school."

"And I'm all alone," Molly said sadly.

It was the first time for Molly without Amy or Lisa. The Three Bears had all been together in kindergarten and first grade. Then in second Molly and Lisa had had Mrs. Brown and Amy had had Mrs. Freemont. And in third and fourth, Amy and Molly had had Mrs. Peabody and Lisa was in the other class. But it was not fair, Molly thought to herself, that this year when everything else was going badly and her brother and sisters had almost left her out completely, she should have her turn to be all alone in the class of the worst teacher in the school.

"I know," Lisa said, but she did not seem to be very interested in Molly's life. Instead she asked Priscilla questions about where she used to go to school before she came to Lake Shore Elementary and how many brothers and sisters she had and did she play sports and was she in the Girl Scouts. Molly listened, sick with jealousy that this new brown-haired baby doll was going to take her place as the baby bear.

When the bell rang for the end of recess, Lisa and Amy jumped up and walked back to the building with Priscilla, the adorable, between them.

"See you after school," they called cheerfully to Molly.

"You should make new friends," Mrs. Lottmann said after Molly had told her the story of Lisa and Amy and Priscilla. "I'm sure there are some terrific children in your class but you've never had a chance to get to know them because you spend all of your time with Lisa and Amy."

"I don't want to get to know them," Molly said. "What I want to do is transfer to Mr. Williams' fifth grade instead," Molly said.

"You can't," Ellie said. "Remember, Mommy, I tried and the principal said no."

"I want to try anyway," Molly said. "I want you to call the school tomorrow morning and tell them. Otherwise I'm not going to school again this year."

"You bet," Benj said.

"You have to go to school, Molly," Ellie said. "It's the law."

"You just wait and see," Molly said. She picked up Morgan and went upstairs to her bedroom, got in her pajamas, brushed her teeth, and crawled under the covers with her old stuffed Easter rabbit and a reluctant Morgan.

"Sick, Moll?" Sarah asked as she went by Molly's bedroom door.

"I think," Molly said.

"What's the matter?" Sarah asked.

"A lot."

Molly wanted Sarah to wait, to come in her room and sit down on her bed and talk for hours and hours without answering the telephone when Josh Truitt called or without doing her French homework or sewing her new skirt for the twelfth-grade dance.

"I feel really terrible," Molly said.

Sarah leaned against the door. "I'm so sorry, Moll. You've been having a very hard time."

"I know," Molly said.

"So you're probably upset, not sick."

"I've been thinking," Molly said.

She had been thinking all day, all summer, really, since things began to change.

"The trouble with being the youngest is that I need everybody more than they need me."

"I need you, Molly," Sarah said.

"You need Josh Truitt and sometimes Benj and even Ellie and Mommy and Daddy. But not me."

"That's not really true," Sarah said, and she had just started to sit down on Molly's bed when the telephone rang and of course it was Josh Truitt and Sarah was gone for the night.

Chapter Three

On the second day of fifth grade, Molly got up, brushed her teeth, put on her red shorts and a Lake Shore Elementary T-shirt, combed her hair, made her bed, and even found both tennis shoes under her dresser where she had kicked them the night before. Morgan lay in a semicircle in the middle of her pillow, where he often settled for the day. Flips lay on the rug in the hall and looked at her with his large and sorrowful eyes. She heard her family at breakfast downstairs. There was the low monotone of Benjamin, Sarah chirping in French, and Mrs. Lottmann talking to Mr. Lottmann with her warm singsong voice.

"Molly?" Mrs. Lottmann called.

Molly sat on the end of her bed and did not answer.

"Breakfast, darling," her mother called again.

Still she did not answer.

Molly heard Benj and Ellie leave for school, arguing as usual. She heard her father's car in the driveway and then she heard the *beep-beep* of Josh Truitt's horn.

"*Au revoir*," Sarah called.

"Molly," Mrs. Lottmann called. "It's almost eight." She started up the stairs.

Molly picked up Morgan, put him under her arm, got down on her hands and knees, and crawled under the bed so she was hidden from view by the rose flounce skirt of her bedspread.

"Molly," Mrs. Lottmann called from the doorway to Molly's bedroom. And then Molly heard the click of her mother's heels cross the hall into her own bedroom.

Molly did not know what she planned to do exactly. She didn't want to go to school to Mrs. P. Lear's class. That was certain. She didn't want to see Amy and Lisa and their new best friend, Priscilla. She didn't want to stay at home all day with no one to speak to but Flips and Morgan, who at that moment lay curled and purring on her stomach.

She could hear her mother on the telephone and then she heard the sharp click of her high heels.

"Mary Christine," she said in quite a cross voice. "I know you're here." She opened the closet door. "Molly?" She was walking around the bedroom. "Please, Molly," she said. And suddenly the rose flounce of the bedspread lifted, and there was her mother, peering under the bed at Molly and Morgan.

"I won't come out," Molly said.

Mrs. Lottmann sat down on the bed.

"How did you know where to find me?" Molly asked.

"You are my daughter," her mother said. "I just knew."

Molly was quiet. She was actually pleased that her mother had found her. What she wanted to do was persuade her mother to stay home from work. They could have breakfast together, maybe croissants at the Bread Oven. Then they'd go to the park and sit on the swings like they used to do when Molly was little. And then they might go to the library, where her mother used to sit at the large table in the center of the room reading magazines while Molly sat on the floor in the children's section and read. She liked feeling as if she were at the library alone and at the same time she could see her mother across the wide room with her magazines, permanent until Molly was ready to go home.

"Do you have to go to work today?" Molly asked from under the bed.

"I don't have to go to work, but obviously I have work to do at my office," her mother said in a reasonable voice.

"But if I asked you to stay home just this once since I don't want to go to school because I hate it, would you do that?"

Mrs. Lottmann hesitated.

Under the bed, Molly waited quietly for her mother's answer.

"I would do that," her mother said finally.

Molly put Morgan on the floor, turned over on her stomach, and crawled halfway out from under the bed. Her mother went into the hall where the telephone was kept. Molly lay on her stomach and listened. First her mother called her office to say that she would not be in to work that day. Then she called Lake Shore Elementary School to say that Molly would not be at school that day. She didn't say that Molly was sick or had a dentist's appointment. She simply said her daughter would not be at school.

Molly got up and combed her black curly hair. "Would you like to go to the Bread Oven for breakfast?" Molly asked her mother.

"That sounds lovely, darling," Mrs. Lottmann said.

"I'd like a chocolate croissant," Molly said.

After the Bread Oven, they went to the park. The day was bright and warm and the park was full of little children with their mothers, playing in the sandbox and on the slides. Molly sat in the swing next to her mother, her feet scraping the dirt, swinging slowly back and forth.

"I feel as if my childhood is gone," Molly said. "I'm not a baby any longer and I'm not grown up." She leaned her head against the swing chain. "I'm just nothing."

Her mother smiled. "What is happening to you isn't easy. But you are becoming somebody other than little Molly Lottmann."

On the way to the library, walking down Clivedon Avenue hand in hand with her

mother, Molly thought about what her mother had said.

She had thought before about becoming somebody very important. Mostly she thought about becoming an Olympic runner because she had watched every minute of the Summer Olympics. She had always been quite a good runner. Even when her legs were short and plump, she had come in second and third after Lisa in the dashes on Blue and White Day at Lake Shore Elementary.

She could imagine herself a runner. She could see herself standing on the winner's block at the Olympics with a gold medal around her neck while the orchestra played "The Star-Spangled Banner" and everybody in the stands cheered and shouted her name.

Besides, no one in the Lottmann family was known as a runner. Sarah was known as a good student and for her art work, particularly her designs for dresses. Benj was known as a baseball player, although according to Ellie he was not very good, and as a basketball player—at that game he was very good and a show-off. Benj was in fact very well known for the wrong reasons, according to Mr. Lottmann. And Ellie was known as an actress. She had been an actress from birth, Mrs. Lottmann said. Even when she didn't have the lead in a school play, she was acting some kind of part, which was the excuse Mrs. Lottmann gave for allowing her to wear purple eye shadow. But so far Molly had only been known as somebody's baby sister.

"I have thought about running in the Olympics," she told her mother. "Nobody in our family has ever thought of that."

"What a good idea, Moll," her mother said. "But you'll have to start at the beginning."

"I have started," Molly said. "I came in third in third grade in the dash. I beat all the girls but Lisa."

"I remember. And now your legs have gotten longer, you could be very good."

They walked up the steps to the library.

"And," her mother said, kissing her youngest daughter's hand, "if you get to be a very fast runner, you'll never have to call out 'wait for me' again because you'll be in the lead."

Chapter Four

On Wednesday, the third day of fifth grade, it rained in gray sheets and the air was chilly. Molly slid under the covers, so her quilt covered her head, and lay very still. From the hall she could hear the bad tempered chatter of Sarah and Ellie and Benjamin getting ready for school.

"Hurry up, Ellie," Sarah called. "My turn in the bathroom."

"I will not hurry up," Ellie said. "Benjamin threw my eye shadow in the toilet."

"By accident," Benjamin yelled. "Ellie always leaves that yucky stuff on the back of the toilet and it fell in by accident."

"You're too young to wear eye shadow," Sarah said in her grandmotherly voice. "No

37

one in seventh grade but Ellie wears eye shadow, Mommy. It's not normal."

"I don't want to be normal," Ellie said. "I want to be an actress. Sandy Pizzo in sixth grade wears eye shadow and she does commercials for Perpetual Bank."

Molly put her pillow over her head. It used to be that everyone would sit in her room in the morning before school and talk pleasantly to one another like children in the movies.

"Good morning, rolly polly Molly," Sarah would call out.

"Morning, Moll," Ellie would say and leap from the door to Molly's bed and tickle her until she was screaming with hysterical delight.

"Hurry up, Moll," Benj would call from downstairs, "and I'll wait for you to walk to school with Petie and me."

That was the way it used to be, when Molly was in the fourth grade.

"Hurry up, Molly," Mrs. Lottmann said, coming into Molly's room and pulling down the covers. "You promised yesterday."

Molly turned over on her back.

"I don't feel well," she said without much certainty.

"You feel fine, Mary Christine," her mother said. "Now get up and ready for school, pronto."

At breakfast her stomach was upset just thinking about Mrs. P. Lear and Lisa and Amy, but her father made her eat.

"Maybe I'll be sick," Molly said.

"You'll be just fine," Mr. Lottmann said. "Finish your cereal and I'll drive you to school today."

She went to the garage through the kitchen door and got into her father's small blue car.

Molly did not usually tell her father very much about her personal life. He was a prosecuting attorney who spent his working day in court with criminals, and worked late in the evening. Nevertheless, this morning he was in a talkative humor and asked her about Lisa and Amy and about the terrible Mrs. P. Lear.

"Mommy told me about your friends leaving

you out," he said. "I know about that feeling. It is really quite awful."

Molly nodded. She was afraid that if she spoke she would start to cry, and she didn't want to cry in front of her father, not now while he was taking her so seriously.

"I'll tell you a story," her father said. "It's about a little boy who was always left behind when his brothers and their friends went off to play baseball.

" 'You're too young,' they had told him. 'You'll get hurt.'

" 'I won't get hurt,' the little boy said.

" 'You'll slow down our game.'

" 'No, I won't,' the little boy said, although he was afraid they might be right.

"So day after day that year between the time he was ten and eleven years old, he practiced pitching a baseball into a circle he had drawn on an elm tree in a field behind his house. By baseball season, the spring of his fifth-grade year, he had become very good at hitting the center of the circle on the tree.

" 'Just once,' he told his brothers that summer when they went out to play baseball. 'Let me try once and I'll never ask you to take me with you again.'

"And reluctantly, the brothers let him go with them to the field where the older boys played baseball.

" 'Let me try to pitch,' he said.

"They laughed at him.

" 'Pitch?' they said. 'You're only ten years old and you can't pitch to guys our age,' they sneered at him.

"But in the end they let him try.

" 'You get to pitch ten balls and that's it,' they said to him. 'That's it forever until you're sixteen.'

" 'Okay,' he agreed, full of confidence.

"He stood on the pitcher's mound and threw. The first ball went directly over home plate.

" 'Lucky,' the boys called.

"The second ball went over home plate.

" 'Strike two!'

"And the third ball.

" 'This can't be all luck,' his brothers said.

" 'We'll let him pitch until he makes mistakes,' one of the older boys said.

"Of course he was wonderful. And they never left him behind again."

"Who was the little boy?" Molly asked.

"Who do you think?"

"I think he was you."

Her father laughed. "Maybe he was me," he said, "and maybe I made him up."

He stopped the car in front of Lake Shore Elementary School and kissed her good-bye.

"I'm sure there's a game of baseball that you can learn to play," he said, and drove off to his office at the courthouse.

Amy stood in her new red pants and shirt at the top of the steps to the school, and Molly's heart leapt up.

"Hello, Moll," Amy called when she saw her. "Where were you yesterday? We had a picnic after school at the playground."

"I was at home," Molly said.

"Sick?"

"Nope. Just home." She sat down on the step next to Amy.

"Where was the picnic?"

"Just under the willow tree. It was Lisa and me and Priscilla. We would have had you if you'd been at school."

Molly hugged her knees under her chin.

"Today we're going to take Priscilla to the library and the duck pond and the stationery store so she'll know her way around town," Amy said. "Maybe you can come."

Amy's voice was perfectly friendly, Molly thought to herself. Just like it had always been. There was no reason, she supposed, to think their friendship was kaput. It just felt that way since Priscilla had arrived at Lake Shore Elementary.

"I don't know if I can go today," Molly said. "I may be going shopping with Ellie." She made that up of course. Ellie would never in a million years go shopping with Molly. At least not lately.

"Maybe we can do something on the weekend," Molly said.

"Like a movie," Amy said.

In the distance, they could see Lisa walking with her little brother and Priscilla James up Alcott Road to the elementary school. "Look who's coming." Amy jumped up.

Molly got up, picked up her bookbag, tossed it over her shoulder, and waved to Amy.

"See you later. Maybe in gym," she called merrily, although she did not feel at all merry.

It was almost time for the bell, and Mrs. P. Lear's fifth-graders were taking their seats when Molly walked into the classroom. She slid into the seat between Tammy Rice and Billy Eaton, who was leaning over his desk making a poster.

She sat down full of purpose. Her mother was right. She would make new friends in fifth grade so she did not have to depend absolutely on Ellie and Sarah and Benj or for that matter on Lisa and Amy. And she would think of something like baseball to be good at just as her father had done when he was ten years old.

Chapter Five

LAKE SHORE ELEMENTARY SCHOOL
BLUE AND WHITE DAY
Friday, September 29
RUN FOR YOUR TEAM
sprinters, long-distance runners,
hurdlers, high jumpers, broad jumpers

"You ought to run for us, Molly," Billy Eaton said to her as they walked down the steps to the playground for recess.

Molly shook her head. "I'm too slow," she said.

"You're a fast runner," Billy said. "I remember in third grade when you beat everyone but Lisa and me at Blue and White Day. Remember that?"

Of course she remembered. She still had the yellow ribbon for third place on the mirror above her dresser. It was the only prize she had ever won.

Lake Shore Elementary was divided into two teams, the Blue Team and the White Team. Molly was a White. So had Sarah and Benjamin and Ellie been Whites. Sarah had been captain of the White Team in sixth grade, and Benjamin had almost been captain, but his best friend Petie had won the year they were in the sixth grade. Ellie had not been anything at all. She did not do sports because, as she told her father when he criticized her for not participating in Blue and White Day, "I always come in last."

"Someone has to come in last," her father said.

"I just don't want to be the one," Ellie said.

But Molly loved Blue and White Day, which was held twice every year, once in September and once in May. There were no afternoon classes those two days, and the teams in each grade competed for points in running and jumping and relays. Molly had never gotten any points for the White Team except the year she won a yellow ribbon in the dash, but Sarah and Benjamin had gotten lots. Twice a year the winning team got its name and captain on the trophy board in the gym, so in 1985 it said, "Sarah Lottmann *Whites.*" And each year the losing team gave the winning team a barbecue on the field behind the elementary school and everybody came, even people who used to go to Lake Shore Elementary.

On Blue and White Day in fourth grade, Molly was home with the chicken pox in September and with strep throat in May. That year Lisa won the fifty- and the hundred-yard dash and the hurdles, and Billy Eaton won the broad jump and came in second in the hundred-yard dash. All during the fourth grade, when the coach had them run dashes in gym class Molly came in fifth or sixth or seventh. Even the smaller children beat her.

"I've gotten much slower this year," she told her mother that year. "I don't think I'll ever win a ribbon on Blue and White Day again."

Nevertheless, since her third-grade victory Molly had imagined herself at Blue and White

Day in the fifth grade, the first year the boys and girls ran separately, winning for her team. And now she knew, in spite of her protests about her slowness, that she was going to sign up to run.

"Did you see the Blue and White Day poster?" Lisa asked Molly on the playground during recess.

"Yes."

"I hope you'll try out this year since you were sick last year. I am. Even Priscilla is going to try out although she's never been in races before."

"I might even do it," Amy said. "Lisa thinks I could do the broad jump. What about you, Moll?"

"Maybe," Molly said.

Already she had imagined herself at the starting line in a white shirt with *Molly Lott-mann* written in blue on the back. She heard the starting gun and the race was on. In her daydream she began slowly but gradually she pulled out ahead, past Amy, past Mary Brewer and Dahlia Furness and Sandra Siller and even

Lisa. Sailing in front. And there were Ellie and Benjamin and Sarah on the sidelines as she crossed over the finish line. She would walk right by Ellie and Benj and Sarah without even a glance in their direction, straight up to the principal, who would pin a blue ribbon on her shoulder.

"Come get ice cream with us to celebrate," Ellie would say.

"I'm too busy to have ice cream with you," Molly would tell her brother and sisters. "Today everybody has invited me for ice cream."

So right after recess, Molly walked straight into the principal's office and signed up to try out for Blue and White Day.

So, she thought to herself, sitting down next to Billy Eaton in art class, she would win a ribbon this year.

Chapter Six

Mrs. P. Lear kept the fifth-grade class after school because Billy Eaton fell over backward in his chair and everybody laughed.

"That's it," Mrs. P. Lear said. "Everyone stays right here in their seats without a word until ten minutes after three."

Then Sally Moss got the hiccups and Jay Cant dropped the pencils from his pencil case, so Mrs. P. Lear added fifteen more minutes. By the time Molly got out of class, packed her bookbag, and raced down the steps, Lisa and Amy were nowhere to be seen. She looked everywhere—all over the school, even the library and the lunchroom and the all-purpose room and on the playground and the lower playing field, but they were not anywhere.

So, she thought, they had gone to show Priscilla around the town of Medford, Massachusetts, without her. She crossed Clivedon Avenue at the light and walked in the direction of Fern Street, where the Lottmann house was third from the corner, painted yellow with black shutters and a black picket fence.

No one would be at home unless Ellie was there. Her mother got home from work at seven with her father. Sarah was probably somewhere with Josh, the creep. Benjamin was at soccer practice and if Ellie were at home now, what good would that do Molly? She would be in her bedroom doing her face with eye makeup or trying on Sarah's clothes.

And then all at once, out of the corner of her eye, she saw Lisa and Amy and Priscilla. They were walking more than a block ahead of her.

"Lisa," she called. She crossed Maple and began to run.

"Lisa!"

No one turned around. Perhaps the traffic was making too much noise for them to hear her.

"Wait for me," she called, already out of breath. "Please wait for me."

But they had not heard her or else they weren't paying attention, so at Fern Street she turned left and headed home.

She took the key from underneath the brick where it was hidden, opened the door to her house, and went inside. Sorrow-eyed Flips lay in the hall, half sleeping, her tail slapping the hardwood floor, pleased with Molly's arrival. Morgan was curled on the hall table under a lamp. Ellie's bookbag had been dropped in the kitchen and all of the contents were spilled out, including two notebooks, a half eaten apple, a Mars bar, a picture of her boyfriend Sean who did not know that he was her boyfriend, a poster of James Dean, and a sweatshirt.

"Hello," Molly called.

There was no answer.

"Hello," Molly called again.

"I'm sleeping," Ellie said.

"Sleeping?" Molly said. She went upstairs. Ellie was in her room under the covers with her door open.

"I'm not sick," Ellie said.

"What's the matter with you?"

"I'm depressed."

Ellie had not volunteered a conversation with Molly for months.

"How come you're depressed?" Molly asked.

"Because Sean"—Ellie sat up in bed—"you know who Sean is?"

"The boy who you have a picture of."

"Right. Sean Peter Mulligan. Five foot six. 130 pounds. Birthday, December 16."

"Yes?"

"Well, he has another girlfriend. He has chosen baby-faced Maripat Freid for a girlfriend."

"I'm really sorry, Ellie."

"Me, too," Ellie said. "I have never been so sorry in my whole life."

"Well, I had sort of the same kind of day, too," Molly began.

Ellie made a face. "You always want to be just like Sarah and me. And you can't, Molly," Ellie said. "You are too young for heartbreak." And she pulled the covers up over her face.

"Nobody is too young for heartbreak," Molly said. Certainly her heart was breaking in pieces all over the place. But she didn't bother to say anything more to Ellie Lottmann, who had gone deaf to any thoughts but the ones she had about herself.

"Just leave me alone," Ellie said. "I'm too depressed. Besides I've changed since last year, and you don't really understand me any longer."

"I hate change," Molly said.

"Well, you'd better get used to it," Ellie said. "You're going to change, too."

"Not me," Molly said, and she jumped down the stairs three steps at a time.

"You, too," Ellie said.

"See you later," Molly said to Ellie.

Maybe she'd go for a bike ride, downtown past the duck pond where Lisa and Amy were playing with Priscilla. "I'm going for a bike ride."

"And leaving me alone?" Ellie said.

But Molly was already out the back door. She took her bicycle out of the garage and rode down Clivedon Avenue.

At Rose Street she turned off and went on the back streets toward town, winding through Rose Park where the houses were small and close together and the yards were full of babies in playpens or strollers or toddling across the grass. The sight of so many babies safe and sound with their mothers, who talked in clusters on the front steps of their houses, made her sad. She remembered feeling just that safe not long ago, even just last year. She hated change. She wanted time to stop six months ago. She wanted for all of the Lottmanns to be like the family in her first-grade reading book, year after year exactly the same.

She crossed Monroe Avenue and rode up on the sidewalk beside Monroe High School, just above the track which was full of runners—mostly boys, but also a few girls and two women who seemed to be older than her mother. She rode down the hill, parked her bike, and sat down on the grass next to a boy maybe as old as Sarah with tight curly red hair and long white legs.

"Hi ya," he said. "Come to run on the track with us?"

"I don't know," Molly said. "I really was just passing by and came down the hill to watch."

"Are you a runner?"

"I'm just in fifth grade," Molly said. "But I was thinking of trying out for Blue and White Day at Lake Shore Elementary."

"Great." The boy stood up and stretched,

bending down to touch his toes. "Yeah, Lake Shore. I went to Lake Shore and was on the White Team."

"Me, too," Molly said, very pleased.

"My name is Jack," the boy said.

"I'm Molly."

"Well, Molly, you had better practice with us for the Whites," the boy said. "Come on. Once around the track with me."

Molly leaned down and tied her tennis shoes tighter.

"I'll try," she said. "I'm really terrible."

"That's okay," the red-haired boy said. "All you need to do is try."

He started to run, but slowly, in step with Molly. "Now you keep up with me," he said.

"What if I can't?"

"You can."

And Molly did. Twice around the track before she collapsed on the grass.

"Had enough?" Jack said.

Molly nodded.

"Well, come back tomorrow and practice with us again. You'll be the best White in the fifth grade."

"Maybe," Molly said. But she was full of

excitement. She jumped on her bicycle and pedaled home as fast as she could. She couldn't wait to tell Sarah and Benj and Ellie that she was training with the Monroe High School Track Team.

Sarah was sitting at the kitchen table, eating carrot sticks, when Molly walked in the back door.

"Guess where I've been?" she said.

"Where?" Sarah asked.

"Running."

"That's great, Moll."

"Not just running either," Molly said. "I've been running with your high school track team. They invited me. They said they needed a mascot and maybe I could be it."

She took six chocolate chip cookies out of the cupboard, poured a glass of milk, and sat down next to Sarah.

"It was funny," she said. "This boy who has bright red hair just sat down with me and made friends like it's perfectly normal to be friends with a fifth-grade girl."

"I bet it's Jack," Sarah said. "Jack Olsson."

"He's really nice."

"That's right," Sarah said. "He's the nicest boy in the high school. You're lucky you met him."

Molly felt very lucky. She went up to her bedroom, shut her bedroom door, and looked at herself in the full-length mirror. Maybe she was changing. She wasn't plump little Molly Lottmann any longer. She was becoming tall and even skinny, and her legs were beginning to look like the legs of a runner.

Chapter Seven

*T*hat night Molly couldn't sleep. It was almost midnight by the bright yellow light of her digital alarm clock. Down the hall the door to her parents' bedroom was closed. Ellie's room was dark but, as usual, music was playing on her tape recorder. On the third floor Benjamin had no doubt been asleep since after dinner.

"I don't know how you are going to get through high school if you can't stay awake long enough to do your homework," Mr. Lottmann said to Benj every night.

Molly got up and wandered into the hall. The light was still on in Sarah's room, and Molly could hear Sarah's soft voice talking to Josh, the creep. Before Josh, Sarah had always had time to talk to Molly, but now if she wasn't flying around Medford, Massachusetts, in Josh's little red car, she was lying on her back with her feet propped up against the wall, talking to him on the telephone.

"Sorry to bother you," Molly said when Sarah hung up.

"S'all right," Sarah said. "He had to hang up."

She got up, took her T-shirt off, dropped her skirt on the floor, put on a nightgown, and climbed under the covers.

"So Moll, what are you doing up this late?"

Molly sat down at the end of her sister's bed.

"I can't sleep," she said. "I have insomnia."

"You're too young for insomnia, Molly," Sarah said. "You must have something else."

"What I have is bad dreams while I'm still awake."

After her trip to the track of Monroe High School, after supper at which Benj was in trouble for a D in a Biology test, after doing the dishes with Ellie, and after doing her own homework in math and kissing her parents good night, Molly crawled into bed with a terrible feeling of loneliness. The feeling was not new, but it was worse. She rolled on her stomach and closed her eyes, but she could not sleep. Spread across the inside of her eyelids was a scene of the Monroe High School track. There were the boys running side by side in white running shorts and blue shirts, and there was Lisa van der Mer running beside Molly. Jack and a few of his friends had stopped running and stood on the side of the track. At first Molly thought they were shouting for her, but as she passed by them she heard Jack say, "Let's go, Lisa. Let's go."

"I'm almost winning," Molly called out. "I'm beating Lisa. Can't you see me?"

But they kept cheering for Lisa as if they could not even see Molly Lottmann.

Every time Molly closed her eyes, the same scene flew into her mind, until finally she didn't even try to sleep any longer.

"Have you ever felt invisible?" Molly asked her older sister. "As if you are there but no one can see you?"

"I don't remember feeling invisible," Sarah said.

"That's probably because you're the oldest. Of course everybody can see you because you came first."

"Everyone can see you too, Molly."

"No," Molly said, flopping down next to Sarah on the bed. "They could when I was little, but now at ten I'm neither little or big. I'm nothing at all but a regular invisible girl."

"*Pauvre petite* Molly." Sarah ruffled her hair.

"I hate it when you speak French," Molly said. "I want our family to stay exactly the same forever with you speaking English."

"I just can't, Moll," Sarah said softly. "Nothing stays the same forever."

"Then I wish everybody would wait for me to catch up."

Sarah brushed Molly's curls off her forehead the way she used to do when Molly was small.

"What I really wish is to be so important and in such a hurry that everybody else would beg me to wait for them."

"That will happen soon, Molly." Sarah reached up and turned off the bedroom light. "You can spend the night if you'd like," Sarah said sleepily.

"Really?"

"Sure." Sarah snuggled next to her younger sister.

"Like we used to do," Molly said.

"Everything won't change, Molly," Sarah said. "Just some things."

*C*hapter *E*ight

*O*n the first day of the second week of fifth grade, Molly started a plan. She wrote it down on construction paper and put it up on the bulletin board over her desk: the Mary Christine Lottmann Plan for fifth grade. She got up early, even before Ellie, who had to get up very early to put on her eye shadow and decide what she was going to wear to school. She took a shower before Sarah so there was hot water left, fed Flips and Morgan, packed her bookbag, made a peanut butter sandwich for lunch, and was sitting at the kitchen table with a bowl of raisin bran when her mother came downstairs in her robe, her hair in electric rollers, to fix breakfast.

"Molly," she said with great pleasure. "You're so organized this morning."

"Not so organized," Molly said, but she was very pleased her mother had noticed.

Upstairs, Benj called down to say he couldn't find his favorite baseball cap and Molly had been the last one to have it.

"Have you seen it, darling?" Mrs. Lottmann asked.

"I wasn't the last one to have it," Molly said. "It's on the hall table where Benj left it last night when Daddy told him he wasn't supposed to wear a hat in the house."

Then Ellie called down to ask who had taken her favorite red sweater, which had been on her closet shelf.

"Molly?" she called crossly.

"Was it you, darling?" Mrs. Lottmann asked. "I know you love that sweater."

"I wouldn't dream of taking stupid Ellie's red sweater," Molly said, putting her backpack over her shoulder. "It isn't always me, just because I'm the youngest."

She kissed her mother good-bye, called good-bye to her father who was in the study reading the morning paper, and waved to Sarah who had just rushed downstairs.

"*Au revoir*," Molly called back.

Molly walked down Fern to Clivedon, then left on Clivedon toward Lake Shore Drive. Billy Eaton rode by on his bicycle and waved.

"Trying out for the track meet?"

"I think."

"Well, you better practice so the Whites can win."

"I will," Molly said.

"See you later, alligator," he called and rode off.

At Alcott, Molly heard Lisa call her. Lisa was running down Alcott, dragging her little brother behind. "Molly," she called.

"Hi," Molly said, a little awkward because their friendship had changed in the last week and she was not at all sure how to behave around Lisa and Amy.

"We've hardly seen you since school started," Lisa said.

"I've been very busy," Molly said. She wanted to say, "I've been left out so of course you haven't seen me, dodo. Ever since baby doll Priscilla arrived." But she didn't want Lisa and Amy to know that her feelings had been hurt.

She wanted them to think that she had not missed them a bit, that she no longer needed them, that she, Molly, Mary Christine Lottmann, was perfectly all right on her own.

"Well, today Amy and I are taking Priscilla to the library and doing our homework there, and then we're going to get a root beer float at Sugar Babies. Maybe you could come?"

"I don't know," Molly said.

"I could help you with your math."

Lisa helped everyone with homework, especially Molly, who was not bad in school necessarily but simply did not like to do her homework. In fourth grade, she had often been unprepared and Lisa had finished her assignments for her. In fact, Molly thought as she walked down Lake Shore Drive next to Lisa, she had never done anything alone. Not even her homework.

"You have to learn to be on your own, Moll," her mother had said to her just last week, the afternoon they had played hooky together. "We haven't been fair to allow you to be a baby for so long."

"Of course it was fair," Molly had said. "And I wish it were true forever."

* * *

"So maybe you can come with us today," Lisa said.

Priscilla stood at the corner of Lake Shore Drive waiting patiently.

"We meet here every morning," Lisa explained. "She still feels a little uncomfortable in Medford."

Priscilla did not seem to Molly to be uncomfortable. She fell in step and chattered with Lisa about the movie they saw together on Saturday and her trip to the beach and the letters she had received from her old best friends in New Jersey where she used to live.

"Now I have new best friends," Priscilla said happily.

Amy was waiting at the front door to Lake Shore Elementary.

"Hi, everybody," she called. "We tried to get you on Saturday to go to the movies, Molly, but Lisa said no one was at home."

But the bell rang for the beginning of school and they all ran off to their classrooms—Lisa and Amy and Priscilla skipping down the corridor to Mr. Williams' class and Molly alone.

"Hi ya, Molly," Sally Kohl said. "We're late."

"Hi," Molly said, very pleased that Sally Kohl, who was the most popular girl in the fifth grade, knew her name. She flopped down in her seat. At recess, she decided during the Pledge of Allegiance, she would make friends with Sally Kohl.

At recess, however, Molly went out on the playground alone. Sally Kohl had to stay in the classroom and talk to Mrs. P. Lear because she had missed too many words on the spelling test. Molly stood at the top of the steps that led to the swings and seesaws and the open fields where the older boys played, where the willow tree spilled its umbrella leaves over the corner where she and Lisa and Amy had played every year since kindergarten. She walked down the stairs looking for Lisa and Amy, but they were not under the tree.

"Hi," she said to a girl in Mr. Williams' class. "Have you seen Lisa van der Mer?"

The girl shook her head.

"I saw her in the library," Billy Eaton said.

"She was with Amy and a new girl in fifth grade who looks like she's three years old."

"I know her," Molly said. "Her name is Priscilla and she's exactly our age."

The boys in the fifth grade were playing touch football on the far field and Billy Eaton ran off to join them, which left Molly standing in the middle of the playground alone. All around her were children in groups of two or three or four, jumping rope or hanging upside down from the jungle gym or playing dodge ball on the asphalt. Three fifth-grade girls she knew slightly lay under the willow tree—telling secrets, she supposed, for that is exactly what she and Lisa and Amy had done. She leaned against the basketball post and pretended to be thinking, so no one would notice that she was alone. If they noticed, then she would certainly be completely alone forever, at least as long as she was in the fifth grade, because no one wants to be with a girl who doesn't have any friends. So she leaned against the basketball post and imagined that she had just won the Olympics as the youngest girl runner in history. Just at

the moment she was picturing the Gold Medal being placed around her neck, Sally Kohl raced up behind her and put her hands over Molly's eyes.

"Guess who?" Sally said.

"I can't," Molly said, although she very much hoped it was Sally Kohl.

"Me," Sally said. "Brother, that was awful. Mrs. P. Lear is going to call my parents because I did so badly on the spelling test, and now I'm going to have to spend every recess learning the words I missed and being tested week after week until I get a ninety."

"I'll help you," Molly said happily. "Spelling is one of the few things in school that is easy for me."

They went off together and collapsed under the willow tree, telling terrible stories about Mrs. P. Lear.

By the time the recess bell rang, Sally Kohl and Molly were friends. They walked back into the building arm in arm. For the first time since the beginning of school, when Molly saw Lisa and Priscilla at the water fountain together she called hello with only a small twinge of sorrow.

*   *   *

When Molly got home from school, Ellie was sitting at the kitchen table in a Lake Shore Raiders sweatshirt, bad tempered with the flu.

"Have you seen my red sweater?" she said crossly.

"I told you no this morning already," Molly said. She took down the bag of chocolate chip cookies from the cupboard and took three. "I don't wear your clothes any longer."

"That's because I won't let you."

"I don't wear them because I like my own clothes better than yours." She poured a glass of milk, took Morgan from the kitchen counter where he was sleeping, and went upstairs.

She changed to shorts and a T-shirt and sneakers. Then she did all of her homework except a composition in English. It was four o'clock. She would just have time to make it to the Monroe High track.

"I'm going on a bike ride and will be back by six," she said to Ellie, still at the kitchen table.

"If I find my red sweater," Ellie said, "you can wear it."

"Thanks, El," Molly said, and she went out the back door, into the garage, hopped on her bike, and rode to Monroe High School.

The boys were there loping around the track, talking back and forth. Several of them were on the hill, including Jack, doing stretching exercises.

"It's Molly," Jack called. "Look, you guys. Molly's here."

"Hi," she said shyly.

"So let's go, Molly," Jack said. "Are you ready?"

"If you go slowly," Molly said, falling in step between Jack and a slight yellow-haired boy not very much bigger than she was.

"It's a mile and a half for you today," Jack said.

"I can't," Molly said. "I did half a mile only yesterday."

"Then one mile," Jack said.

"Don't think about it," the yellow-haired boy said. "It will be by in a flash."

"Hi, Molly," a group of boys waved as they went by her.

79

"Hi," she called back, feeling important. Jack and the yellow-haired boy kept even with her. From time to time Jack said "Great going, Molly."

And the mile was over—four times around the track. She had hardly noticed it.

"So you see," Jack said, "you're in great shape."

She laughed. She was tired but she felt wonderful. She lay down on the grassy hill beside the track and looked at the falling sun. She felt better than she had felt since school started—almost as happy as she used to feel before everybody grew up and left her behind.

Chapter Nine

Lisa and Amy and Priscilla had become a group—a tight little group. Molly saw them ahead of her as she walked to school, their heads together, giggling. She saw them at recess lying on their stomachs under the willow. If they saw her, they waved and called for her to come on over and talk, but usually they saw only one another. They left school together, and Molly would see them walking arm in arm down Clivedon Avenue on their way to the library. Lisa had stopped calling on the telephone at dinner time. Amy didn't invite her to go to the movies at her father's theater.

"It isn't fair," Molly said to her mother.

"No, it isn't," her mother said. "Things aren't always fair."

"You always say that. It doesn't help," Molly said. "I wish we would move to Boston."

"Then you wouldn't have a chance to run on Blue and White Day."

"Who cares?" Molly said.

But she was beginning to care very much.

Every day at the track she met the boys from Monroe High School, and they were always glad to see her. She didn't know most of their names, except Jack of course, but they knew hers.

"Let's go, Moll-ee," they'd shout.

"Don't tire out on us, Molly. You can keep up with the boys."

They timed her on the fifty-yard dash and the hundred.

"Okay, Molly," Jack would say. "Let's see if you can beat yesterday's time."

Most days after practice, one of the boys would buy her a fruitstick from the Good Humor man.

"For running so well today," they'd tell her.

Her times got better and better, though not every day. One day, she was recovering from the stomach flu and another she was too tired because she had stayed up late to watch a special on TV. But there was steady improvement.

She was becoming friends with Sally Kohl. Sally had three friends in Mrs. P. Lear's class whom Molly had always known, though she had never been friends with them. The five of them spent recess together and sat at the same table at lunch. She was invited to Sally's birthday party in late September, which was a sleepover.

It wasn't that Lisa and Amy didn't speak to her. They did. But things between them were different.

"I wasn't unkind when Lisa and I were in the same class, or Amy and I," she said to her mother.

"Tell them, darling. If they are really unkind, you should not put up with it," Mrs. Lottmann said.

But they were not really unkind. They were simply preoccupied with each other, and Molly didn't belong any longer. Or at least that was the way she felt.

* * *

In her daydreams, it was September 29 and she and Lisa were dressing in the locker room for Blue and White Day.

"Good luck," Lisa said.

"Thanks," Molly said. "You too."

Molly pulled her hair back in a rubber band; she and Lisa went out to the track together. The class was already lining up—Sally Kohl and Mary Truitt and Christy Best and Sandy Siller and Franny Take. Molly took her place on the outside and Lisa stepped in the middle between Christy Best and Sandy Siller. In the race as she imagined it, Molly was always behind at first and then she got a second wind and sailed past Lisa, who was sometimes disqualified for falling and sometimes simply didn't run fast.

Blue and White Day got closer and closer. At recess and after school the field of Lake Shore Elementary was full of children practicing. There were high spirits and excitement, with bake sales and car washes to make money for the cookout afterward, and banners for the teams and the best athletes.

Go Billy Go was hung in red letters in the hallway outside Mrs. P. Lear's classroom.

Lisa, Lisa, She's Our Girl hung over the door of Mr. Williams' classroom.

Yea Blues, Yea Whites hung on every available bulletin board.

There wasn't a sign for Molly Lottmann. No one expected her to win.

Chapter Ten

*F*riday afternoon was cold and damp and gray, but everyone at Lake Shore Elementary School was outside in shorts and T-shirts with *White* or *Blue* on the back, shivering as they waited their turn. All the teachers were there, as well as brothers and sisters and mothers and fathers, and older boys and girls who had graduated, even grown-ups who had long before gone to Lake Shore Elementary School. Blue and White Day was a very big deal.

The day had not gone at all well for Molly Lottmann. First she couldn't find her math homework paper and Mrs. P. Lear accused her of not doing her work at all. At noon she dropped one of her tennis shoes into the trash bin with her empty lunch bag, so when the bell rang for Blue and White Day she couldn't find one of her tennis shoes in her locker. If it had not been for the janitor, who emptied the trash at the exact right moment, her shoe might have been gone forever. And then as she raced down the back steps of the school building, late for the beginning of the track meet, she fell down the last few steps and twisted her ankle.

Lisa stood on the other side of the playground with Mr. Williams and waved to Molly as she passed.

"Are you doing the fifty and the hundred?" she called to Molly.

Molly nodded.

"Good luck," Molly said.

"I always hate to run against you," Lisa said.

'So do I," Molly agreed, but actually, as she walked across the field to the place where Mrs. P. Lear's fifth grade was standing, she was glad to be running against Lisa. She was glad for the chance to win.

The gym teacher blew the whistle for fifth-grade races.

"I'm so nervous," Sally Kohl said. "I couldn't eat all day."

"Line up behind your captains," the gym teacher said.

Molly stood behind Sally. She didn't talk. Her ankle hurt. She could feel that it was beginning to swell, and her stomach was flip-flopping.

"Are your parents here?" Sally asked.

'They're coming."

"I think I see your brother."

Molly scanned the crowd.

"I don't think so," she said.

"I saw him ride up on his bike."

"Fifth-grade girls' fifty-yard dash," the coach called out above the scattered voices. "Line up."

"So these are the rules," the coach said. "I'll say *on your mark*. Then I'll wait to see if you're all ready. Then I'll say *get set*. And then the gun will go off. At the gun, you'll run as fast as you can to the string, which you won't be able to see from the starting line. And don't slow down until you go through the string. Understand?"

Suddenly Molly saw Benjamin standing by his bicycle, with his baseball cap pulled down over his eyes as usual, and next to him were

Sarah and Ellie and her mother and father. It made her heart beat double-time just to see them there.

"On your mark," the coach called.

Molly wiped her damp hands on her shorts. She leaned slightly forward and put her weight on her left leg as she had seen the athletes do in the Olympics.

"Get set," the coach shouted.

Molly's mouth was dry. She felt as if she were going to faint.

And the gun sounded.

Molly started. She could feel the whole line of fifth-grade girls burst out in front of her but she looked straight ahead at the invisible string that marked the finish line.

Her legs began to feel lighter, to move faster, and as she ran the tension that had made her breath come in short takes fell away. She pulled ahead of Sally Kohl, who ran beside her, and then Eve Shakel. She felt herself go faster and faster, even now with Mary Truitt and Christy Best. She pushed herself harder, closer and closer to Lisa, and without even realizing that she had broken the string, she crossed the finish line. The crowd was cheering.

She couldn't tell who had won although she knew it was close.

"Number three," the coach shouted, "Mary Truitt."

"Number two," she said, "Lisa van der Mer."

"And first prize in the fifth-grade girls' fifty-yard dash," she said, "Molly Lottmann."

Chapter Eleven

The sun fell and darkness came quickly with the cold. The sky was wide and sprinkled with stars. Molly lay on Sarah's lap between Lisa and Amy, her eyes closed, lulled by the sound of familiar voices.

At the ceremony she had stood next to Lisa and Mary Truitt while the principal pinned their ribbons on their shoulders. Yellow for Mary, red for Lisa, and blue for Molly. It was not as exciting as her daydreams of the Olympics, of course, but it was exciting, and when the principal came to Molly, she said, "And who would have thought little Molly Lottmann was going to grow up this year."

Everybody cheered and Molly could hear Benj in the background shouting, *"Yeah, Molly!"*

"That was an amazing run," Lisa said on their way back from the awards ceremony. "Have you been practicing?"

"Sort of," Molly said.

"I practiced every day with Amy timing me. Even on the weekends. Who did you practice with?"

"Mostly I practiced alone," Molly said. They sat down to watch the other awards together.

"Now that Blue and White Day is over, maybe you'll have more time to do things with Amy and me."

"What about Priscilla?"

"And Priscilla." Lisa was pensive. "I like Priscilla," she said. "I mean we both like Priscilla, but it hasn't been the same without you."

Molly didn't say anything, but inside she was bursting with joy.

At eight, after the cookout and the singing was over, Mr. Lottmann said it was time to go home. So Molly hugged Lisa good-bye and she hugged Amy good-bye and she helped her father fold the blanket where they'd been sitting. Arm in arm, she walked to the car between Sarah and Ellie.

"So Molly," Benj was saying. "Petie was there and so was Ray and they thought you were just great."

"You were," Sarah said. "I was so proud of you."

Molly ducked under Sarah's arm, pulled away from Ellie, and ran through the darkness to the lot where the car was parked.

"Hurry up," she called when she had reached the car. "Hurry up, you guys. It's late."